archys life of mehitabel

by

don marquis

faber & faber limited
3 queen square
london

first published in 1934
by faber and faber limited
3 queen square london wc1
first published in this edition 1961
reprinted 1965, 1969 and 1973
printed in great britain
by r maclehose and company limited glasgow
all rights reserved

isbn 0 571 06616 x

archy s life of mehitabel

by the same author

*

archy and mehitabel

contents

chapter		page
	introduction	7
i.	the life of mehitabel the cat	11
ii.	the minstrel and the maltese cross	13
iii.	mehitabels first mistake	17
iv.	the curse of drink	21
v.	pussy café	25
vi.	a communication from archy	29
vii.	the return of archy	33
viii.	archy turns highbrow for a minute	37
ix.	archy experiences a seizure	39
x.	peace—at a price	45
xi.	mehitabel again	51
xii.	archy among the philistines	53
xiii.	archy protests	57
xiv.	CAPITALS AT LAST	59
xv.	the stuff of literature	61
xvi.	archys autobiography	63
xvii.	quote and only man is vile quote	65
xviii.	mehitabels morals	69
xix.	cream de la cream	73
xx.	do not pity mehitabel	77
xxi.	mehitabel tries companionate marriage	79
xxii.	no social stuff for mehitabel	83
xxiii.	the open spaces are too open	87
xxiv.	random thoughts by archy	91

contents

chapter		page
xxv.	archy turns revolutionist	95
xxvi.	archys last name	101
xxvii.	quote buns by great men quote	103
xxviii.	archys song	105
xxix.	an awful warning	107
xxx.	as it looks to archy	111
xxxi.	archy a low brow	115
xxxii.	archy on the radio	117
xxxiii.	mehitabels parlour story	125
xxxiv.	archys mission	127
xxxv.	archy visits washington	131
xxxvi.	ballade of the under side	135
xxxvii.	archy wants to end it all	139
xxxviii.	book review	143
xxxix.	archy and the old un	145
xl.	archygrams	149
xli.	archy says	155
xlii.	sings of los angeles	157
xliii.	wants to go in the movies	159
xliv.	the retreat from hollywood	163
xlv.	artists shouldnt have offspring	167
xlvi.	what does a trouper care	169
xlvii.	is a coyote a cat	171
xlviii.	human nature aint that bad	173
xlix.	could such things be	175
l.	be damned mother dear	177
li.	the artist always pays	179
lii.	maternal care	183
liii.	to hell with anything common	185
liv.	a word from little archibald	191

Introduction

Archy the Cockroach made his initial appearance in my office a good many years ago, in fact about the same time that free verse began to commend itself to the multitudes because it looked as if it would be so easy to write. There was a period which many persons still more or less alive may remember when you could not scratch a taxi-driver, an insurance agent, or a newspaper reporter without finding a free-verse poet under the skin. Archy claimed that he was a victim of transmigration; that he had been a *vers libre* bard, and that for his sins of omission and commission his soul had been sentenced to serve an indeterminate sentence in the body of a cockroach. Mehitabel the Cat, who appeared about the same time, made a similar claim; before she was Mehitabel, she said, she had been Cleopatra and various other lively ladies.

Archy writes without punctuation because he is forced to use his head to butt the keys of the typewriter one at a time, and he is not able to reach the shift keys of the machine in order to make punctuation marks or capital letters. Mehitabel does not use the typewriting machine at all, so Archy is forced to be her reporter.

introduction

I must suppose that these creatures have a kind of vitality. During the eight or ten years in which they appeared in the New York *Evening Sun*, and the several years succeeding in which they contaminated the pages of the New York *Herald Tribune* and the twenty-odd other journals throughout the country to which the material was syndicated, I tried to kill them off at least half a dozen times. But they would not stay dead. Every time I killed them, I got hundreds of letters from their devoted readers demanding an immediate resuscitation. It was easy enough to manage these resurrections; every time I stepped on Archy and slew him, his soul could transmigrate into another cockroach without missing a strophe. I finally began to understand that for some reason or other (or possibly for no reason at all) there was a certain public which wanted them. A few years ago I collected a number of Archy's communications into a book, and this volume surprised me by selling thirty thousand copies at a time when "books were not selling". The characters appeared for two years in *Colliers' Weekly* also, and they must have met with a response in that journal, for the editors insisted that I do them every week. For these reasons, it seems worth while to get out another book.

DON MARQUIS

archy s life of mehitabel

archy s life of mehitabel

i
the life of mehitabel the cat

boss i am engaged on a literary
work of some importance it is
nothing more nor less
than the life story of
mehitabel the cat she is
dictating it a word
at a time and all
the bunch gather around to listen but
i am rewriting it as i go along
boss i wish we
could do something
for mehitabel she is

a cat that has seen
better days she has
drunk cream at fourteen
cents the half pint
in her time and now she
is thankful for a
stray fish head from a
garbage cart but she is
cheerful under it all toujours
gai is ever her word
toujours gai kiddoo drink she
says played a great
part in it all she
was taught to drink
beer by a kitchen maid she
trusted and was
abducted from a luxurious home
on one occasion in a
taxicab while under
the influence of beer which
she feels certain had been
drugged but still her
word is toujours gai my
kiddo toujours gai wotto hell
luck may change

                                    archy

ii
the minstrel and the maltese cross

well boss i promised to tell you
something of the life story of
mehitabel the cat archy says she i
was a beautiful kitten and as good
and innocent as i was beautiful my
mother was an angora you dont
look angora i said your fur
should show it did
i say angora said mehitabel it must
have been a slip of the tongue my
mother was high born and of
ancient lineage part persian and part

maltese a sort of maltese cross
i said archy she said please
do not josh my mother i
cannot permit levity in connection
with that saintly name she knew many
troubles did my mother and
died at last in a slum far from
all who had known her in her better
days but alas my father
was a villain he too had noble blood
but he had fallen into dissolute
ways and wandered the
alleys as the leader of a troupe of
strolling minstrels stealing milk
from bottles in the early mornings
catching rats here there and
everywhere and only too frequently
driven to the expedient of dining on
what might be found in
garbage cans and suburban
dump heaps now and
then a sparrow or a robin fell to my
fathers lot for he was a mighty hunter i
have heard that at times he even
ate cockroaches and as she said
that she spread
her claws and looked at me with her
head on one side i got into the works
of the typewriter mehitabel i

said try and conquer that wild and
hobohemian strain in your blood archy
she said have no fear i have dined
today but to resume my
mother the pampered beauty that she
was was eating whipped cream one
day on the back
stoop of the palace where she resided
when along came my father bold
black handsome villain that he was and
serenaded her his must have been a
magnetic personality for in spite of
her maiden modesty and
cloistered upbringing she responded
with a few well rendered musical
notes of her own i
will not dwell upon the wooing suffice
it to say that ere long they
not only sang duets together but
she was persuaded to join
him and his troupe of strollers in
their midnight meanderings alas that
first false step she
finally left her luxurious home it was
on a moonlight night in may i have
often heard her say and again and
again she has said to me that she
wished that robert w chambers could
have written her story or maybe john

galsworthy in his later and
more cosmopolitan manner well to
resume i was born in a stable in
greenwich village which was at
the time undergoing transformation
into a studio my
brothers and sisters were drowned
dearie i often look back on my life and
think how romantic it has all
been and wonder what fate saved
me and sent my brothers and sisters
to their watery grave archy i
have had a remarkable life go
on telling about it i said never
mind the side remarks i became
a pet at once continued
mehitabel but let us not make the first
instalment too long the
tale of my youth will be reserved
for your next chapter to be continued
                                    archy

iii
mehitabels first mistake

well i said to
mehitabel the cat continue
the story of your life i
was a pampered kitten for
a time archy she said but
alas i soon
realized that my master and
mistress were becoming
more and more fond of a
dog that lived with
them in the studio he was
an ugly mutt take it from

me archy a red eyed little bull
dog with no manners i
hope i was too much of a lady
to show jealousy i have
been through a great deal
dearie now up and now down
but it is darn seldom
i ever forget i was a
lady always genteel archy
but this red eyed mutt was
certainly some pill and those
people were so stuck on
him that it would have made
you sick they called him
snookums and it was snookums
this and snookums that and
ribbons and bells and porterhouse
steak for him and if he
got a flea on him they called a
specialist in only one
day archy i hear my
mistress say snookums ookums
is lonely he ought to
have some one to play with
true said her husband every
dog should be brought up along
with a baby a dog
naturally likes a child to
play with we will have no

children said she a
vulgar foolish little child
might harm my snookums we
could muzzle the child said
her husband i am sure
the dog would like one to
play with and they
finally decided they would get
one from a foundling home
to play with snookums if
they could find a child
with a good enough pedigree
that wouldnt give any
germs to the dog well
one day the low lived mutt
butted in and tried to
swipe the cream i was drinking even
as a kitten archy i
never let any one put anything
across on me although i
am slow in starting
things as any real lady
should be dearie i let
this stiff snookums get
his face into the saucer
and then what i did
to his eyes and nose with
my claws would melt the
heart of a trained

nurse the simp had no
nerve he ran to his
mistress and she came after
me with a broom i
got three good scratches
through her silk stockings
archy dearie before i
was batted into the
alley and i picked myself
up out of a can full
of ashes a cat without a
home a poor little
innocent kitten alone
all alone in the great and
wicked city but i never
was one to be down
on my luck long archy my
motto has always been
toujours gai archy toujours
gai always jolly archy
always game and thank god
always the lady i
wandered a block or
two and strayed into
the family entrance of
a barroom it was my
first mistake mehitabels
adventures will be continued
                              archy

iv

the curse of drink

to continue the story
of mehitabel the cat
she says to me when i
walked into that
barroom i was hungry and
mewing with despair
there were two men sitting
at the table and
looking sad i rubbed
against the legs of one
of them but he never moved
then i jumped up on

the table and stood
between them they both stared
hard at me and
then they stared at each
other but neither one
touched me or said anything
in front of one of
them was a glass full
of some liquid with
foam on the top of it i
thought it was milk
and began to drink from the
glass little did i
know archy as i lapped
it up that it was beer the
men shrank back from me and
began to tremble and shake
and look at me
finally one of them said to
the other i know what you
think bill what do i
think jeff said the
other you think bill that
i have the d ts said the
first one you think i
think i see a cat drinking
out of that beer glass but
i do not think i
see a cat at all that is all

the curse of drink

in your imagination it
is you yourself that
have the d ts no said the
other one i dont think
you think you see a
cat i was not thinking
about cats at all i
do not know why you mention
cats for there are no
cats here just then a
salvation army lassie came
in and said you
wicked men teaching that poor
little innocent cat to
drink beer what cat
said one of the men she
thinks she sees a cat
said the other and
laughed and laughed
just then a mouse ran
across the floor and i
chased it and the salvation
lassie jumped on a
chair and screamed jeff
said bill i suppose now you
think i saw a
mouse i wish bill you
would change the
subject from animals said

jeff there is nothing
to be gained by talking
of animals mehitabels
life story will be
continued in an early number
                    archy

v

pussy café

for some weeks said
mehitabel the cat continuing the
story of her life i
lived in that barroom and
though the society was
not what i had
been used to yet i
cannot say that it was
not interesting three
times a day in
addition to scraps from
the free lunch

an an occasional mouse
i was given a saucer
full of beer sometimes i
was given more and
when i was feeling
frolicsome it was the custom
for the patrons to gather
round and watch me
chase my tail until
i would suddenly fall
asleep at that time
they gave me the
nickname of pussy café but
one day i left the
place in the pocket
of a big fur
overcoat worn by
a gentleman who was
carrying so much that i thought
a little extra burden would
not be noticed he got
into a taxi cab
which soon afterwards
pulled up in front of
a swell residence uptown
and wandered up the
steps well said his
wife meeting him in the
hallway you are here

pussy café

at last but where is my
mother whom i sent you to
the train to meet
could this be she asked
the ladys husband
pulling me out of his
coat pocket by the neck and
holding me up with a
dazed expression on his face
it could not said his
wife with a look of
scorn mehitabels life
story will be continued
before long

                          archy

vi

a communication from archy

well boss i am
sorry to report that
mehitabel the cat has
struck no more story archy
she said last night
without pay art for arts
sake is all right but
i can get real
money in the movies the
best bits are to
come too she says my life
she says has been a

romantic one boss she has
the nerve to hold out
for a pint of
cream a day i am sick
of milk she says and
why should a lady author
drink ordinary milk cream
for mine she says
and no white of egg beaten
up on top of it either i
know what my dope
is worth boss it is
my opinion she has the
swell head over getting into
print i would hate
to stop the serial
but she needs a
lesson listen archy she said
to me what i want
with my stuff is
illustrations too the next
chapter is about me taking
my first false step well
archy i either get an
illustration for that or else
i sign up with these
movie people who are always
after me you will be
wanting to sing into a phonograph

next i told her
my advice is to
can her at once i will fill
the space with my own
adventures

           archy

vii

the return of archy

where have i been so long
you ask me
i have been going up
and down like the devil
seeking what i might devour
i am hungry always hungry
and in the end i shall
eat everything
all the world shall come at
last to the multitudinous maws
of insects
a civilization perishes

before the tireless teeth
of little little germs
ha ha i have thrown off the mask
at last
you thought i was only
an archy
but i am more than that
i am anarchy
where have i been you ask
i have been organizing the insects
the ants the worms the wasps
the bees the cockroaches
the mosquitoes
for a revolt against mankind
i have declared war
upon humanity
i even i shall fling
the mighty atom
that splits a planet asunder
i ride the microbe
that crashes down olympus
where have i been you ask me where
i am jove and from my seat
on the edge of a bowl of beef stew
i launch the thunderous
molecule
that smites a cosmos into bits
where have i been you ask
but you had better ask

the return of archy

who follows in my train
there is an ant
a desert ant a tamerlane
who ate a pyramid in rage
that he might get at and devour
the mummies of six hundred
kings who in remote
antiquity had stepped upon
and crushed ascendants of his
my myrmidons
are trivial things
and they have always ruled
the world
and now they shall strike down mankind
i shall show you how
a solar system
pivots on the nubbin
of a flageolet bean
i shall show you how a blood clot
moving in a despots brain
flung a hundred million men
to death and disease
and plunged a planet into woe
for twice a hundred years
we have the key
to the fourth dimension
for we know the little things
that swim and swarm
in protoplasm

i can show you love and hate
and the future
dreaming side by side
in a cell
in the little cells where
matter is so fine it merges
into spirit
you ask me where i have been
but you had better
ask me where i am
and what
i have been drinking
exclamation point

                              archy

viii

archy turns highbrow for a minute

boss please let me
be highbrow for
a minute i
have just been eating
my way through some of
the books on your desk
and i have digested two of them
and it occurs to me
that antoninus the emperor
and epictetus the slave
arrived at the same
philosophy of life

that there is neither mastery
nor slavery
except as it exists
in the attitude of the soul
toward the world
thank you for listening
to a poor little
cockroach

                    archy

ix
archy experiences a seizure

"Where have you been so long? And what on earth do you mean by coming in here soused?" we asked Archy as he zigzagged from the door to the desk.

He climbed onto the typewriter keys and replied indignantly:

      soused yourself i havent had a drink
      and yet i am elevated i admit it i have
      been down to a second hand book
      store eating a lot of kiplings earlier
      poetry it always excites me if i eat
      a dozen stanzas of it i get all lit up

and i try to imitate it get out of my
way now i feel a poem in the kipling
manner taking me

And before we could stop him he began to butt
on the keys:

    the cockroach stood by the mickle
       wood in the flush of the astral dawn

We interrupted. "Don't you mean Austral instead of astral?"
Archy became angered and wrote peevishly:

    i wrote astral and i meant astral
    you let me be now i want to get this
    poem off my chest you are jealous if
    you were any kind of a sport at all
    you would fix this machine so i could
    write it in capitals it is a poem about
    a fight between a cockroach and a
    lot of other things get out of my way
    im off

    the cockroach stood by the mickle
       wood in the flush of the astral dawn
    and he sniffed the air from the hidden
       lair where the khyber swordfish spawn

archy experiences a seizure

and the bilge and belch of the glutton
    welsh as they smelted their warlock cheese
surged to and fro where the grinding
    floe wrenched at the headlands knees
half seas over under up again
and the barnacles white in the moon
the pole stars chasing its tail like a pup again
and the dish ran away with the spoon

the waterspout came bellowing out of
    the red horizons rim
and the grey typhoon and the black
    monsoon surged forth to the
    fight with him
with three fold might they surged to
    the fight for they hated the great
    bull roach
and they cried begod as they lashed
    the sod and here is an egg to
    poach
we will bash his mug with his own raw
    lug new stripped from off his
    dome
for there is no law but teeth and claw
    to the nor nor east of nome
the punjab gull shall have his skull
    ere he goes to the burning ghaut
for there is no time for aught but crime
    where the jungle lore is taught

across the dark the afghan shark is
   whining for his head
there shall be no rule but death and
   dule till the deep red maws are
   fed
   half seas under up and down
   again
   and her keel was blown off in a
   squall
   girls we misdoubt that we ll ever
     see town again
   haul boys haul boys haul.

"Archy," we interrupted, "that haul, boys, is all
right to the eye, but the ear will surely make it hall
boys. Better change it."

you are jealous you let me alone im off again

the cockroach spat and he tilted his
   hat and he grinned through the
   lowering mirk
the cockroach felt in his rangoon belt
   for his good bengali dirk
he reefed his mast against the blast
   and he bent his mizzen free
and he pointed the cleats of his bin
   nacle sheets at the teeth of the
   yesty sea

he opened his mouth and he sluiced
   his drouth with his last good
   can of swipes
begod he cried they come in pride but
   they shall go home with the
   gripes

begod he said if they want my head it
   is here on top of my chine
it shall never be said that i doffed my
   head for the boast of a heathen
   line
and he scorned to wait but he dared
   his fate and loosed his bridle rein
and leapt to close with his red fanged
   foes in the trough of the
   screaming main
from hell to nome the blow went home
   and split the firmament
from hell to nome the yellow foam
   blew wide to veil the rent
and the roaring ships they came to
   grips in the gloom of a dripping
   mist

'Archy," we interrupted again, "is there very
much more of it? It seems that you might tell in a
very few words now who won the fight, and let it go
at that. Who did win the fight, Archy?"

But Archy was peeved, and went sadly away, after writing:

of course you wont let me finish i never saw as jealous a person as you are

x

peace—at a price

one thing the human
bean never seems to
get into it is the
fact that humans
appear just as unnecessary to
cockroaches as cockroaches
do to humans
you would scarcely
call me human
nor am i altogether
cockroach i
conceive it to be my

mission in life to bring
humans and cockroaches
into a better understanding
with each other to
establish some sort of
entente cordiale or
hands across the kitchen sink
arrangement
lately i heard a number
of cockroaches discussing
humanity one big
regal looking roach
had the floor and he spoke
as was fitting in blank verse
more or less
says he
how came this monster with the heavy
foot harsh voice and cruel heart to
rule the world
had it been dogs or cats or elephants
i could have acquiesced and found a
justice working in the decree but man
gross man
the killer man the bloody minded
crossed unsocial death dispenser of this
sphere who slays for pleasure slays
for sport for whim
who slays from habit breeds to slay and
slays

whatever breed has humors not his own
the whole apparent universe one sponge
blood filled from insect mammal fish
and bird
the which he squeezes down his vast
gullet friends i call on you to rise and
trample down this monster man this
tyrant man hear hear said
several of the wilder spirits
and it looked to me for a
minute as if they
were going right out and
wreck new york city but
an old polonius looking
roach got the floor
he cleared his throat three times
and said
what our young friend here
so eloquently counsels against
the traditional enemy is
calculated of course to appeal to
youth what he says
about man is all very true
and yet we must remember that
some of our wisest
cockroaches have always
held that there
is something impious in the
idea of overthrowing man

doubtless the supreme being
put man where he is and
doubtless he did it
for some good purpose which
it would be very
impolitic yea well nigh
blasphemous for us to enquire
into the project of
overthrowing man is indeed
tantamount to a
proposition to overthrow the
supreme being himself and
i trust that no one of
my hearers is so wild or
so wicked as to think
that possible or desirable i
cannot but admire the
idealism and patriotism of
my young friend who
has just spoken nor do i
doubt his sincerity but i
grieve to see so
many fine qualities
misdirected and i
should like to ask him
just one question to wit
namely as follows is it not
a fact that just before
coming to this meeting

he was almost killed by a
human being as he
crawled out of an ice box
and is it not true that
he was stealing food from
the said ice box and is it
not a fact that his own
recent personal experience has
as much to do with
his present rage as any
desire to better the
condition of the cockroaches of
the world in general
i think that it is the sense of
this meeting that a
resolution be passed censuring
mankind and at the
same time making it
very clear that nothing like
rebellion is to be attempted
and so on
well polonius had his way
but it is my belief that the
wilder spirits will gain the
ascendancy and if the
movement spreads to the other
insects the human race is in
danger as a friend of both
parties i should regret war

what we need is
intelligent propaganda who is
better qualified to handle
the propaganda fund than
yours truly

            archy

xi
mehitabel again

well boss mehitabel the
cat is sore at me she says
that it was my fault
that you cut off her story
of her life right in
the middle and she
has been making my life a
misery to me three
times she has almost clawed
me to death i wish
she would eat a poisoned
rat but she wont she

is too lazy to catch one well
it takes all sorts of
people to make an
underworld

                    archy

xii
archy among the philistines

i wish i had more human society
these other cockroaches here are just cockroaches
no human soul ever transmigrated into them
and any soul that would go into one of them
after giving them the once over
would be a pretty punk sort of a soul
you cant imagine how low down they are with no
esthetic sense and no imagination or anything like
that and they actually poke fun at me because i
   used to
be a poet before i died and my soul migrated into a
cockroach they are as crass and philistine as some

humans i could name their only thought is food but
there is a little red eyed spider lives behind your
steam radiator who has considerable sense
i dont think he is very honest though i dont know
whether he has anything human in him or is just
spider i was talking to him the other day and was
quite charmed with his conversation
after you he says pausing by the radiator
and i was about to step back of the radiator ahead
of him when something told me to watch my step
and i drew back just in time
to keep from walking into a web
there were some cockroach legs and wings
still sticking in that web
i beat it as quickly as i could up the wall
well well says that spider you are in quite a hurry
    archy
ha ha so you wont be at my dinner table today then
some other time cockroach some other time
i will be glad to welcome you to dinner archy
he is not to be trusted but he is the only insect
i have met for weeks that has any intelligence if
    you
will look back of that locker where you hang your
hat you will find a dime has rolled there i wish you
would get it and spend it for doughnuts a cent at a
    time
and leave the doughnuts under your typewriter i get
    tired

of apple peelings i nearly drowned in your ink well
   last
night dont forget the doughnuts

                     archy

We are trying to fix up some scheme whereby Archy can use the shift keys and thus get control of the capital letters and punctuation marks. Suggestions for a workable device will be thankfully received. As it is Archy has to climb upon the frame of the typewriter and jump with all his weight upon the keys, a key at a time, and it is only by almost incredible exertions that he is able to drag the paper forward so he can start a new line.

xiii

archy protests

say comma boss comma capital
i apostrophe m getting tired of
being joshed about my
punctuation period capital t followed by
he idea seems to be
that capital i apostrophe m
ignorant where punctuation
is concerned period capital n followed by
o such thing semi
colon the fact is that
the mechanical exigencies of
the case prevent my use of

all the characters on the
typewriter keyboard period
capital i apostrophe m
doing the best capital
i can under difficulties semi colon
and capital i apostrophe m
grieved at the unkindness
of the criticism period please
consider that my name
is signed in small
caps period

                    archy period

xiv

CAPITALS AT LAST

I THOUGHT THAT SOME HISTORIC DAY
SHIFT KEYS WOULD LOCK IN SUCH A WAY
THAT MY POETIC FEET WOULD FALL
UPON EACH CLICKING CAPITAL
AND NOW FROM KEY TO KEY I CLIMB
TO WRITE MY GRATITUDE IN RHYME
YOU LITTLE KNOW WITH WHAT DELIGHT
THROUGHOUT THE LONG AND LONELY
NIGHT
I'VE KICKED AND BUTTED (FOOT AND
BEAN)
AGAINST THE KEYS OF YOUR MACHINE

TO TELL THE MOVING TALE OF ALL
THAT TO A COCKROACH MAY BEFALL
INDEED IF I COULD NOT HAVE HAD
SUCH OCCUPATION I'D BE MAD
AH FOR A SOUL LIKE MINE TO DWELL
WITHIN A COCKROACH THAT IS HELL
TO SCURRY FROM THE PLAYFUL CAT
TO DODGE THE INSECT EATING RAT
THE HUNGRY SPIDER TO EVADE
THE MOUSE THAT %) ?)) " " " $$$ ((gee boss
what a jolt that cat mehitabel made
a jump for me
i got away but she unlocked the shift key
it kicked me right into the
mechanism where she
couldn't reach me it
was nearly the death of little
archy that kick spurned me right
out of parnassus back into
the vers libre slums i lay
in behind the wires for an hour after
she left before i dared to get
out and finish i hate
cats say boss please lock the shift
key tight some night
i would like to tell the story of
my life all in capital
letters

archy

XV
the stuff of literature

thank your friends for me for
all their good advice about how to
work your typewriter but what i have
always claimed is that manners and methods
are no great matter compared
with thoughts in poetry you cant hide
gems of thought so they wont flash
on the world on the other hand if you press
agent poor stuff that wont make it live
my ego will express itself in spite of
all mechanical obstacles having something
to say is the thing being sincere
counts for more than forms of expression thanks
for the doughnuts

archy

xvi
archy s autobiography

if all the verse what i have wrote
were boiled together in a kettle
twould make a meal for every goat
from nome to popocatapetl
mexico

and all the prose what i have penned
if laid together end to end
would reach from russia to south bend
indiana

but all the money what i saved
from all them works at which i slaved

is not enough to get me shaved
every morning

and all the dams which i care
if heaped together in the air
would not reach much of anywhere
they wouldnt

because i dont shave every day
and i write for arts sake anyway
and always hate to take my pay
i loathe it

and all of you who credit that
could sit down on an opera hat
and never crush the darn thing flat
you skeptics
                              archy

xvii

quote and only man is vile quote

as a representative
of the insect world
i have often wondered
on what man bases his claims
to superiority
everything he knows he has had
to learn whereas we insects are born
knowing everything we need to know
for instance man had to invent
airplanes before he could fly
but if a fly cannot fly
as soon as he is hatched

his parents kick him out and disown him
i should describe the human race
as a strange species of bipeds
who cannot run fast enough
to collect the money
which they owe themselves
as far as government is concerned
men after thousands of years practice
are not as well organized socially
as the average ant hill or beehive
they cannot build dwellings
as beautiful as a spiders web
and i never saw a city
full of men manage to be as happy
as a congregation of mosquitoes
who have discovered a fat man
on a camping trip
as far as personal beauty
is concerned who ever saw
man woman or child
who could compete with a butterfly
if you tell a dancer
that she is a firefly
she is complimented
a musical composer
is all puffed up with pride
if he can catch the spirit
of a summer night full of crickets
man cannot even make war

with the efficiency and generalship
of an army of warrior ants
and he has done little else
but make war for centuries
make war and wonder
how he is going to pay for it
man is a queer looking gink
who uses what brains he has
to get himself into trouble with
and then blames it on the fates
the only invention man ever made
which we insects do not have
is money and he gives up
everything else to get money
and then discovers that it is not worth
what he gave up to get it
in his envy he invents
insect exterminators
but in time every city he builds
is eaten down by insects
what i ask you is babylon now
it is the habitation of fleas
also nineveh and tyre
humanitys culture consists
in sitting down in circles
and passing the word around
about how darned smart humanity is
i wish you would tell
the furnace man at your house

to put out some new brand
of roach paste i do not get
any kick any more out of the brand
he has been using the last year
formerly it pepped me up
and stimulated me
i have a strange tale about
mehitabel to tell you
more anon

          archy

xviii

mehitabel s morals

boss i got
a message from
mehitabel the cat
the other day
brought me by
a cockroach
she asks for our help
it seems she is being
held at ellis
island while an
investigation is made
of her morals

she left the country
and now it looks as
if she might not
be able to get
back in again
she cannot see
why they are
investigating
her morals she says
wotthehellbill she says
i never claimed
i had any morals
she has always regarded
morals as an unnecessary
complication in life
her theory is
that they take up room that might
better be devoted to
something more interesting
live while you are alive
she says and postpone
morality to the hereafter
everything in its place
is my rule she says
but i am liberal she
says i do not give
a damn how moral other
people are i never try
to interfere with them

in fact i prefer them
moral they furnish
a background for my
vivacity in the meantime
it looks as if she
would have to swim
if she gets ashore and
the water is cold

                    archy

xix

cream de la cream

well boss mehitabel the cat
has turned up again after a long
absence she declines
to explain her movements but she
drops out dark hints of a
most melodramatic nature ups and downs
archy she says always ups and downs
that is what my life has
been one day lapping
up the cream de la cream and the
next skirmishing for
fish heads in an alley but

toujours gai archy toujours gai no
matter how the luck broke i have had a
most romantic life archy talk
about reincarnation and transmigration
archy why i could tell you things of who
i used to be archy that would make
your eyes stick out like a snails one
incarnation queening it with a tarara on
my bean as cleopatra archy and
the next being abducted as a poor
working girl but toujours gai archy toujours
gai and finally my soul has migrated to
the body of a cat and not even a persian or
a maltese at that but where have you been
lately mehitabel i asked her never mind
archy she says dont ask no questions
and i will tell no lies all i
got to say to keep away
from the movies have you been in the
movies mehitabel i asked her never mind
archy she says never mind all i got to
say is keep away from those
movie camps theres some mighty
nice people and animals connected with them
and then again theres some that aint i
say nothing against anybody archy i am
used to ups and downs no matter
how luck breaks its toujours gai
with me all i got to say

cream de la cream

archy is that sometimes a cat
comes along that is a perfect gentleman and
then again some of the slickest furred ones
aint if i was a cat that was the
particular pet of a movie star archy and
slept on a silk cushion and had
white chinese rats especially
imported for my meals i would try to live
up to all that luxury and be a
gentleman in word and deed mehitabel i said
have you had another unfortunate romance i am
making no complaint against any
one archy she says wottell archy wottell even
if the breaks is bad my motto is toujours gai
but to slip out nights and sing and frolic
under the moon with a lady and then cut her
dead in the day time before your rich
friends and see her batted out of a studio
with a broom without raising a paw for her
aint what i call being a
gentleman archy and i am
a lady archy and i know a gentleman when
i meet one but wottell archy wottell toujours
gai is the word never say die
archy its the cheerful heart that wins all i
got to say is that if i ever get that
fluffy haired slob down on the
water front when some of my garg
is around he will wish he had

watched his step i aint vindictive archy i
dont hold grudges no lady does but i
got friends archy that maybe would take it
up for me theres a black cat with one ear
sliced off lives down around old slip is a
good pal of mine i wouldnt want to
see trouble start archy no real lady
wants a fight to start over her but
sometimes she cant hold her friends back
all i got to say is that boob with his silver
bells around his neck better sidestep old slip
well archy lets not talk any more about my troubles
does the boss ever leave any pieces of sandwich
in the waste paper basket any more honest
archy i would will myself to a furrier for a
pair of oysters i could even she says eat you
archy she said it like a joke but there
was a kind of a pondering look in her eyes
so i just crawled into the inside of
your typewriter behind the wires it
seemed safer let her hustle for a
mouse if she is as hungry as all that
but i am afraid she never will she
is too romantic to work

                                        archy

XX

do not pity mehitabel

do not pity
mehitabel
she is having
her own kind of
a good time
in her own way
she would not
understand any other
sort of life
but the life
she has chosen
to lead

she was predestined
to it as the
sparks fly upward
chacun à son gout
as they say in france
start her in
as a kitten
and she would
repeat the same story
and do not overlook
the fact that
mehitabel is really
proud of herself
she enjoys
her own sufferings
                archy

xxi

mehitabel tries companionate marriage

boss i have seen mehitabel the cat
again and she has just been through
another matrimonial experience
she said in part as follows
i am always the sap archy
always the good natured simp
always believing in the good intentions
of those deceitful tom cats
always getting married at leisure
and repenting in haste
its wrong for an artist to marry
a free spirit has gotta

live her own life
about three months ago along came a
maltese tom with a black heart and
silver bells on his neck and says
mehitabel be mine
are you abducting me percy i asks him
no said he i am offering marriage
honorable up to date
companionate marriage
listen i said if its marriage
theres a catch in it somewheres
ive been married again and again
and its been my experience
that any kind of marriage
means just one dam kitten after another
and domesticity always ruins my art
but this companionate marriage says he
is all assets and no liabilities
its something new mehitabel
be mine mehitabel and i promise
a life of open ice boxes
creamed fish and catnip
well i said wotthehell kid
if its something new i will take a
chance theres a dance or two
in the old dame yet
i will try any kind of marriage once
you look like a gentleman to me percy
well archy i was wrong as usual

mehitabel tries companionate marriage

i wont go into details for i aint
any tabloid newspaper
but the way it worked out was i rustled
grub for that low lived bum for two
months and when the kittens came
he left me flat and he says these
offsprings dissolves the wedding
i am always the lady archy
i didn t do anything vulgar
i removed his left eye with one claw
and i says to him if i wasn t an
aristocrat id rip you
from gehenna to duodenum
the next four flusher that
says marriage to me
i may really lose my temper
trial marriage or companionate
marriage or old fashioned american
plan three meals a day marriage
with no thursdays off
they are all the same thing
marriage is marriage
and you cant laugh that curse off
                              archy

xxii

no social stuff for mehitabel

i said to mehitabel
the cat i suppose you are
going to the swell cat
show i am not archy
said she i have as
much lineage as any
of those society
cats but i never could
see the conventional
social stuff archy
i am a lady
but i am bohemian

83

too archy i
live my own life
no bells and pink
ribbons for me
archy it is me for
the life romantic i could
walk right into
that cat show and get
away with it
archy none of those
maltese princesses has
anything on me in the
way of hauteur
or birth either or any
of the aristocratic
fixings and condiments
that mark the
cats of lady clara
vere de vere but
it bores me archy
me for the
wide open spaces the
alley serenade and
the moonlight
sonata on the back
fences i would
rather kill my own
rats and share
them with a

friend from greenwich
village than lap up
cream or beef juice
from a silver porringer
and have to
be polite to the
bourgeois clans
that feed me
wot the hell i
feel superior to that
stupid bunch me
for a dance
across the roofs when
the red star
calls to my blood
none of your
pretty puss stuff for
mehitabel it would
give me a grouch
to have to be so
solemn toujours
gai archy toujours
gai is my
motto

                archy

xxiii

the open spaces are too open

boss i saw mehitabel
the cat yesterday she is
back in town after
spending a couple
of weeks
in the country
archy she says to me
i will never leave the
city again no
matter what the weather
may be me for the
cobble stones and the

asphalt and the friendly
alleys the great open
spaces are all right but
they are too open i have been
living on a diet of
open spaces the country is
all right if you have a trained
human family to rustle
up the eats for you or know
a cow who has the
gift of milking herself for
your benefit but archy
i am a city lady
i was never educated to dig for
field mice and as for calling
birds out of the trees i dont
have the musical
education for it i cant
even imitate a cat bird
i will take my chance
hereafter with the garbage
cans in town until
such times as i decorate
a rubbish heap myself
that may not be long archy
but wot the hell
i have had a good time while
i lasted come easy go easy
archy that is my motto

i tried to snatch a bone
from a terrier a month
ago and the beast bit my front
paw nearly off
but wot the hell archy
wot the hell i can still
dance a merry step or two
on three legs i am
slightly disabled archy but
still in the ring and still
i have the class wot the
hell archy i am always
a lady and always gay
and i got one eye out of
that terrier at that
i would be afraid that
mehitabel s end is not far off
if she had not been looking
as bad as she does for
at least three years
she says it is her
romantic disposition
that keeps her young
and yet i think if some
cheerful musical family
in good circumstances were to
offer mehitabel a home
where she would be treated in
all ways as one of the family

she has reached the point where
she might consent to give up
living her own life
only three legs archy she says
to me only three legs left
but wot the hell archy
there s a dance in the old
dame yet

> archy

xxiv
random thoughts by archy

one thing that
shows that
insects are
superior to men
is the fact that
insects run their
affairs without
political campaigns
elections and so forth

*   *   *

a man thinks
he amounts to a lot

91

but to a mosquito
a man is
merely
something to eat

*   *   *

i have noticed
that when
chickens quit
quarrelling over their
food they often
find that there is
enough for all of them
i wonder if
it might not
be the same way
with the
human race

*   *   *

germs are very
objectionable to men
but a germ
thinks of a man
as only the swamp
in which
he has to live

*   *

a louse i
used to know

told me that
millionaires and
bums tasted
about alike
to him

           ★   ★   ★

the trouble with
most people is
that they
lose their sense of
proportion
of what use is
it for a
queen bee to fall in
love with a bull

           ★   ★   ★

what is all this mystery
about the sphinx
that has troubled so many
illustrious men
no doubt the very same
thoughts she thinks
are thought every day
by some obscure hen
                         archy

archy turns revolutionist

if all the bugs
in all the worlds
twixt earth and betelgoose
should sharpen up
their little stings
and turn their feelings loose
they soon would show
all human beans
in saturn
earth
or mars
their relative significance

among the spinning stars
man is so proud
the haughty simp
so hard for to approach
and he looks down
with such an air
on spider
midge
or roach
the supercilious silliness
of this poor wingless bird
is cosmically comical
and stellarly absurd
his scutellated occiput
has holes somewhere inside
and there no doubt
two pints or so
of scrambled brains reside
if all the bugs
of all the stars
should sting him on the dome
they might pierce through
that osseous rind
and find the brains at home
and in the convolutions lay
an egg with fancies fraught
which
germinating rapidly
might turn into a thought

might turn into the thought
that men
and insects are the same
both transient flecks
of starry dust
that out of nothing came
the planets are
what atoms are
and neither more nor less
man s feet have grown
so big that he
forgets his littleness
the things he thinks
are only things
that insects always knew
the things he does
are stunts that we
don t have to think to do
he spent a score
of centuries
in getting feeble wings
which we instinctively
acquired
with other trivial things
the day is coming
very soon
when man and all his race
must cast their silly
pride aside

and take the second place
i ll take the bugs
of all the stars
and tell them of my plan
and fling them with
their myriad stings
against the tyrant man
dear boss this outburst
is the result
of a personal insult
as so much verse always is
maybe you know how
that is yourself
i dropped into an irish
stew in a restaurant
the other evening
for a warm bath and a bite
to eat and a low browed
waiter plucked me out
and said to me
if you must eat i will
lead you to the
food i have especially prepared
for you and he took me
to the kitchen
and tried to make me
fill myself with
a poisonous concoction
known cynically as roach food

archy turns revolutionist

can you wonder
that my anger
against the whole human
race has blazed forth in
song when the revolution
comes i shall
do my best to save
you you have so many
points that are far
from being human

archy

xxvi
archy s last name

boss i just discovered what
my last name is i
pass it on to you i belong to the
family of the blattidae right o
said mehitabel the cat when i told her
about it they have
got you sized up right you blatt out
everything you hear
i gleaned the information from
a bulletin issued by the
united states department of
agriculture which you left on the

floor by your desk it was entitled
cockroaches and written by
e l marlatt entomologist and acting
chief in the absence of the chief and he
tells a dozen ways of killing roaches boss
what business has the united states
government got
to sick a high salaried
expert onto a poor little roach
please leave me some
more cheerful literature also please
get your typewriter fixed the keys are
working hard again butting them as i
do one at a time with
my head i get awful pains in my
neck writing for you

                    archy

xxvii
quote buns by great men quote

one of the most
pathetic things i
have seen recently
was an intoxicated person
trying to fall
down a moving stairway
it was the escalator at
the thirty fourth street
side of the
pennsylvania station
he could not fall down as
fast as it

carried him up again but
he was game he kept on
trying he was
stubborn about it
evidently it was a part of
his tradition habit and
training always to fall down
stairs when intoxicated and
he did not intend to
be defeated this time i
watched him for an hour
and moved sadly away thinking
how much sorrow
drink is responsible for the
buns by great men
reached and kept
are not attained
by sudden flight but they
while their companions slept
were falling upwards
through the night

                                        archy

xxviii
archy s song

man eats the big fish
the big fish eat the
little fish
the little fish
eat insects
in the water
the water insects
eat the water plants
the water plants
eat mud
mud eats man
my favorite poem

is the same as
abraham lincolns
o why should the spirit
of mortal be proud
awaiting your answer
i am and so forth

archy

xxix
an awful warning

dear boss i was walking along
the curbstone yesterday
and i ran sprang into an old bum
who was sitting happily
in the gutter singing
in part as follows

oh i ruined my prospects
by wicked desires
which i put into action
as far as i could
but now i ve arrived

within sight of hell fires
and i wish i d done better
i wish i d been good

as i sit in the gutter
and look at the sky
the man in the moon
is a looking at me
and i thinks to myself
i d have risen that high
if i had behaved myself
proper as he

now all you young fellows
and pretty young janes
as passes me by
and dont pitch me a dime
take warning by me
and avoid all the pains
which comes from remorse
in the fullness of time

and all you young fellows
thats out on a bust
and lively young flappers
so spic and so span
i oncet had a sweetheart
and me she did trust
to maintain myself always
a proper young man

an awful warning

i was lured to a barroom
and there i was tempted
for the bartender cried
be a man and drink rum
and after that first
glass of liquor i emptied
i found myself jobless
and went on the bum

now all you young fellows
and flappers so gay
that passes me by
and dont toss me a cent
there oncet was a time
when i went on my way
with ladylike janes
like an elegant gent

now i sits in the gutter
and looks at the stars
and wish i had always
behaved and been good
and never drunk rum
at them elegant bars
and never been wicked
as much as i could

you gents and your girl friends
should tip an old man

for his horrid example
of not being good
you must try and behave
in so far as you can
you should toss me a dime
for my warning you should

                    archy

XXX

as it looks to archy

ants go on their cheerful way
merrily from day to day
building cities out of sand
and they seem to understand
dwelling therein peacefully
disciplined and orderly
and the much lauded bee contrives
for to fill his thundering hives
with a ranked society
based on work and honesty
and a thousand neat examples
could i cite of insect lives
free from much that tears and tramples

human beings and their wives
even the coral in the ocean
throughout his dim and damp existence
scorns political commotion
and labours with a glad persistence
worthy of large commendations
to erect his naval stations

man the universal simp
follows lagging with a limp
treading on his neighbours toes
the way the little insect goes
in a million years or more
man may learn the simple lore
of how the bees are organized
and why the ants are civilized
may even hope for to approach
the culture of an average roach
if he is humble and not smug
may emulate the tumble bug

for we insects now inherit
all humanity has builded
all they raised with brawn and spirit
all the domes and spires they gilded
time the anthropophagous
swallows down all human works
through his broad esophagus
moslems christians hindus turks

as it looks to archy

pass to their sarcophagus
leaving nothing much on earth
which even beetles find of worth
i mention nineveh and tyre
i cite the tower of babel
troy which fell into the fire
and sodom with its rabble
where are all the towns of siddim
where the kings of crete
long long since the desert hid em
and the spiders bite their feet
following an old convention
dating back to jeremiah
i might even mention
babylon i might enquire
where o where is babylon
and the echo answers where
for its former ruling wizards
sleep in sand and silicon
with gravel in their gizzards
and sand burrs in their hair
and the centipedes are dancing
in the chambers of the palace
where the kings and queens entrancing
used to quaff the ruby chalice
and proceed to their romancing

i look forward to the day
when the human race is done

and we insects romp and play
freely underneath the sun
and no roach paste is scattered
about anywhere i got another jolt of it
last night and today i seem to have a case
of intestinal flu the trouble with you
human beings is you are just plain wicked
                                        archy

xxxi
archy a low brow

boss i saw a picture
of myself in a paper
the other day
writing on a typewriter
with some of my feet
i wish it was as easy
as that what i have to do
is dive at each key
on the machine
and bump it with my head
and sometimes it telescopes
my occiput into my

vertebrae and i have a
permanent callous
on my forehead
i am in fact becoming
a low brow think of it
me with all my learning
to become a low brow
hoping that you
will remain the same
i am as ever your
faithful little bug

           archy

xxxii
archy on the radio

dear boss
i hope you tuned in
last evening when mars and i
were on the radio together
our first joint appearance
in several years

do you realize said mars
that next week will be archy week
all over mars
and several other prominent planets

archy
good gracious mars it had slipped
my memory

mars
do you know that you are
our favorite author here and
we all but worship you

archy
well mars as far as that goes
you are one of my favorite planets

mars
what a coincidence

archy
the long arm of coincidence
makes many radio connections

mars
is that your own phrase archy

archy
mine until the next air programme
nowadays an author owns his stuff
only between air programmes

mars
did you know about the archy clubs here

archy on the radio

archy
i hope they can t throw them this far
what do they look like

mars
like dumbbells ha ha ha
but please tell us how you happened
to start your career as a writer

archy
it did not happen it was something
i planned deliberately so i could quit
being what i was

mars
explain please the stars are listening

archy
well you see i was the four marx brothers
and it became annoying because
i quarrelled among myself all the time
so in order to end it all i turned
author writing dante s inferno and
mehitabel the cat

mars
what do you call that little planet
where you are at

archy
well now what do you call it

mars

we call it goofus

archy

goofus goofus why goofus

mars

not long ago one of our prominent
scientists got a good look at it
with a new fangled telescope and
he laughed himself to death crying out
goofus goofus goofus all the time
he said from the way it looked it couldn t
be named anything else but goofus

archy

well if that s the way you feel who was
the lady i seen you walking with last sunday

mars

that wasn t no lady that was venus
is there any particular message
you would like to send your billions
and billions of admirers in these parts

archy

oh yes tell them
this hour is by the courtesy
of the knockem cold roach and bug killing company

and that i wish to testify
that their product has several times
brought me personally nearer the great adventure
than any other roach paste i ever ate
i always carry a flask of bath tub gin with me
as an antidote

                    mars
will you describe yourself for your
worshipers here

                    archy
i am over six feet and go everywhere

                    mars
who has influenced you most in a
literary way

                    archy
theodore dreiser and bernard shaw
they taught me how far an author can go
if he never loses patience with himself

                    mars
archy it is impossible that you should
not lose patience with yourself sometimes

                    archy
well i havent gone as far as they have either

                    121

mars
what are the conditions of life on your planet archy

archy
they practically dont exist any more

mars
but how do people get along

archy
the men make a living by talking
about how much they have lost
during the depression
and the women and children pick up
what they can by listening
how is it by yourself old timer

mars
we never had to do any work here
we get our living by biting electrons out of the air
which we crack with our teeth
and eat the kernels while we spit
the shells into space which accounts
for a lot of the static you hear

archy
that not only interests me as a scientist
but it seems much more refined than
working for a living

archy on the radio

mars
yes it is refined all right but it is
expensive it runs into terrible dentists bills

archy
but dentists bills are always terrible
everywhere anyhow

mars
wait till i write that down please
do you have to think a long time
for those brilliant things
or do they just come to you

archy
i never think at all when i write
nobody can do two things at the same time
and do them both well

mars
are you starting any new literary movements on
your planet

archy
oh yes the latest literary movement
consists in going to all the fences
and coal sheds near all the school houses
and copying off of them all the bad words
written there by naughty little boys

over the week ends
and these form the bases of the new novels
of course these novels are kept away
from the young so they will not be contaminated

mars
but where do the boys get the words

archy
from hired hands and the classics

archy

xxxiii

mehitabel s parlour story

    boss did you
    hear about the two drunks
    who were riding in
    a ford or something
    equally comic
    and the ford or
    whatever it was nearly
    went off the
    road one of
    the drunks poked the
    other and said thickly
    they always talk thickly in

these stories
anyway he said hey look
out how youre driving
youll have us in
the ditch in a minute if
you dont look out
why said the second
drunk who was drunker
i thought you
were driving i got
that from mehitabel the
cat its the first parlour
story ive ever heard
her tell and ive known
her for five or six
years now
                    archy

xxxiv

archy s mission

well boss i am
going to quit living
a life of leisure
i have been an idler
and a waster and a
mere poet too long
my conscience has waked up
wish yours would do the same
i am going to have
a moral purpose in my life
hereafter and a cause
i am going to reclaim

cockroaches and teach them
proper ways of living
i am going to see if i cannot
reform insects in general
i have constituted
myself a missionary
extraordinary
and minister
plenipotentiary
and entomological
to bring idealism to
the little struggling brothers
the conditions in the insect
world today would shock
american reformers
if they knew about them
the lives they lead
are scarcely fit to print
i cannot go into
details but the contented
laxness in which i find
them is frightful
a family newspaper is no place
for these revelations
but i am trying to have
printed in paris
for limited circulation
amongst truly earnest
souls a volume which will

archy s mission

be entitled
the truth about the insects
i assure you there is nothing
even in the old testament
as terrible
i shall be the cotton mather
of the boll weevil

                    archy

archy visits washington

washington d c july
2 3 well boss here
i am in washington
watching my step for fear
some one will push me
into the food bill up
to date i am the only thing
in this country that
has not been added to it by
the time this is
published nothing that
i have said may be

true however which is a
thing that is constantly happening
to thousands of
great journalists now in
washington it is so hot here that
i get stuck in the asphalt
every day on my
way from the senate press
gallery back to
shoemakers where the
affairs of the nation
are habitually settled by
the old settlers it
is so hot that you can
fry fish on the
sidewalk in any part of
town and many people
are here with fish to fry
including now
and then a german
carp i am lodging on
top of the washington
monument where i can
overlook things
you cant keep a good bug
from the top of
the column all the time i
am taking my meals with
the specimens in the

archy visits washington

smithsonian institution when i
see any one coming i hold
my breath and look like another
specimen but in the
capitol building there
is no attention paid to me
because there are so
many other insects
around it gives you a
great idea of the
american people when you
see some of the
things they elect after july
27 address me care
st elizabeth hospital
for the insane i am going out
there for a visit with
some of your other
contributors

                      archy

xxxvi
ballade of the under side

by archy
the roach that scurries
skips and runs
may read far more than those
that fly
i know what family skeletons
within your closets
swing and dry
not that i ever
play the spy
but as in corners
dim i bide

i can t dodge knowledge
though i try
i see things from
the under side

the lordly ones the
haughty ones
with supercilious
heads held high
the up stage stiff
pretentious guns
miss much that meets
my humbler eye
not that i meddle
perk or pry
but i m too small
to feel great pride
and as the pompous world
goes by
i see things from
the under side

above me wheel
the stars and suns
but humans shut
me from the sky
you see their eyes as pure
as nuns
i see their wayward

136

ballade of the under side

feet and sly
i own and own it with
a sigh
my point of view
is somewhat wried
i am a pessimistic
guy
i see things from the
under side

l envoi
prince ere you pull a bluff
and lie
before you fake
and play the snide
consider whether
archy s nigh
i see things from
the under side

xxxvii
archy wants to end it all

well boss from time
to time i just simply
get bored with having
to be a cockroach my
soul my real ego if
you get what i mean is
tired of being shut
up in an insects body the
best you can say for it is that it
is unusual and you could
say as much for mumps so
while feeling gloomy the

other night the thought came
to me why not
go on to the next stage as
soon as possible why not
commit suicide and
maybe be reincarnated in
some higher form of life why
not be the captain of my
soul the master of my fate and
the more i pondered over it the
more i was attracted to
the notion well boss you would
be surprised to find
out how hard it is for a
cockroach to commit suicide unless
you have been one
and tried it of course i
could let mehitabel the
cat damage me and die that
way but all my finer sensibilities
revolt at the idea i jumped out
the fourth story window and
a wind caught me and blew
me into the eighth story i
tried to hang myself with a
thread and i am so light i
just swung back and forth and
didnt even choke myself shooting
is out of the question and poison

archy wants to end it all

is not within
my reach i might drown myself
in the ink well but if
you ever got a mouthful of it you
would know it was a
thing no refined person could go
on with boss i am going to
end it all before long and i
want to go easy have you
any suggestion yours
for transmigration

                            archy

xxxviii
book review

boss a new book
has appeared
which should be
read by every one
it is entitled
the cockroach
its life history
and how to deal
with it and
the author
is frederick laing
who is assistant

in the department
of entomology in the
british museum
of natural history
it is one of the
best books i ever
tasted i am eating
the binding from
a copy with
a great deal of
relish and
recommend it
to all other
insects yours
truly

       archy

xxixx
archy and the old un

one of the saddest
creatures i ever saw
was a turtle who said
he was a thousand
years old
no turtle looks very
joyous the style of
architecture peculiar
to the faces and necks of
turtles is such
that even if they were to
feel gay internally
they would find difficulty

in expressing their joy
a kind of melancholy dwells
in the wrinkles of a
turtles neck the only thing
that looks sadder than a turtle
is the little dead fish
that is served in an italian
tabledhote restaurant
well this turtle i am telling you
about was so old that
he used to be a pet
of charlemagne
and he finally committed suicide
he stood on his hind
legs and jumped up
and bit himself on the
forehead and held on until
he died
i wrote a poem
about this turtle
after his death
which goes as follows
why did he die perhaps he knew
too much about
the ways of men and turtles
he had seen too much no doubt

optimist in youth of course
youth never quails

archy and the old un

he preached to all his brother turtles
moral turtles turn to whales

but the weary ages passed
and he perceived
turtles still continued turtles
then he doubted disbelieved

brooding for two hundred years
in discontent
he became a snapping turtle
savage cynic in his bent

timon of the turtle tribe
so he withdrew
from the world remarking often
piffle there is nothing true

nothing changes all the salt
that used to be
scattered widely through the ocean
still gives flavour to the sea

nothing changes all the bunk
of long ago
still is swallowed by the nations
progress always stubs its toe

the moral well the morals quite
an easy one

do not live to be a thousand
youll be sorry ere youre done

the only way boss
to keep hope in the world
is to keep changing its
population frequently
i am sorry to be so
pessimistic today
but you see i need a change
very badly
when do we start
for hollywood
i am eager to be gone
i wish to cheer myself
up in some fashion
your faithful little
cockroach

         archibald

xl
archygrams

*   *   *

the wood louse sits on a splinter
and sings to the rising sap
aint it awful how winter
lingers in springtimes lap

*   *   *

it is a good
thing not to be too
aristocratic
the oldest and
most pedigreed
families in this

149

country are the
occupants of various sarcophagi
in the museums
but it is dull associating
with mummies no
matter how royal their
blood used to be when
they had blood
it is like living in
philadelphia

*   *   *

honesty is a good
thing but
it is not profitable to
its possessor
unless it is
kept under control
if you are not
honest at all
everybody hates you
and if you are
absolutely honest
you get martyred.

*   *   *

as i was crawling
through the holes in
a swiss cheese

150

the other
day it occurred to
me to wonder
what a swiss cheese
would think if
a swiss cheese
could think and after
cogitating for some
time i said to myself
if a swiss cheese
could think
it would think that
a swiss cheese
was the most important
thing in the world
just as everything that
can think at all
does think about itself

*   *   *

these anarchists that
are going to
destroy organized
society and civilization
and everything remind
me of an ant i
knew one time
he was a big red ant a
regular bull of an

ant and he came bulging down a
garden path and ran
into a stone gate post curses on
you said the ant to the
stone gate post get out of my
way but the stone never budged
i will kick you over
said the ant and he kicked but
it only hurt his hind legs
well then said
the ant i will eat you down and
he began taking little bites
in a great rage maybe i said
you will do it in
time but it will
spoil your digestion first

*   *   *

a good many
failures are happy
because they don t
realize it many a
cockroach believes
himself as beautiful
as a butterfly
have a heart o have
a heart and
let them dream on

*   *   *

boss i believe
that the
millennium will
get here some day
but i could
compile quite a list
of persons
who will have
to go
first

        *   *   *

tis very seldom i have felt
drawn to a scallop or a smelt
and still more rarely do i feel
love for the sleek electric eel

        *   *   *

the oyster is useful in his fashion
but has little pride or passion

        *   *   *

when the proud ibexes start from sleep
in the early alpine morns
at once from crag to crag they leap
alighting on their horns
and may a dozen times rebound
ere resting haughty on the ground
i do not like their trivial pride
nor think them truly dignified

        *   *   *

did you ever
notice that when
a politician
does get an idea
he usually
gets it all wrong

*   *   *

xli
archy says

one queer thing about
spring gardens is
that so many people
use them to
raise spinach in
instead of food

      *   *   *

everybody has two kinds of friends
one kind tries to run
his affairs for him
and the other kind

well i will be darned if i can remember
the other kind

      *   *   *

now and then
there is a person born
who is so unlucky
that he runs into accidents
which started out to happen
to somebody else

      *   *   *

xlii
sings of los angeles

boss i see by
the papers there
has been more than
one unconventional
episode
in the far west
and i have made
a little song
as follows
los angeles
los angeles
the home of the movie star

what kind of angels
are they
out there where you are
los angeles
los angeles
much must be left
untold
but science says
that freuds rush in
where angels
fear to tread
los angeles
los angeles
clean up your
movie game
or else o city of angels
you better
change your name
yours for all the morality
that the traffic
will bear

                              archy

xliii

wants to go in the movies

boss i wish you would
make arrangements to put me
into the movies a
lot of people who are no
handsomer in the face than i
am are drawing millions of
dollars a year i
have always felt that i
could act if i
were given the chance and a
truly refined cockroach might

be a novelty but do not pay
any attention to the
wishes of mehitabel the cat along
this line mehitabel
told me the other day that several
firms were bidding against
each other for her
services i would be the greatest
feline vamp in the
history of the screen said
mehitabel wot the hell archy
wot the hell ain t i a
reincarnation of cleopatra and
dont the vamp stuff come quite
natural to me i will say it
does but i have refused all
offers archy up to
date they must pay me
my price the
truth is that mehitabel hasnt a
chance and she is not a
steady character by the way
here is a piece of political news
for you mehitabel tells me that
the cats in greenwich
village and the adjoining
neighbourhoods are forming soviets now
they are going in for bolshevism
her soviet she says

wants to go in the movies

meets in washington mews
they are for the nationalization
of all fish markets

archy

xliv
the retreat from hollywood

Archy, the Free Verse Cockroach, and Mehitabel the
Cat, are on their way back from Hollywood, hitch-hiking.
Mehitabel was forcibly ejected at least twice from every
moving-picture studio in Hollywood, and nourishes animos-
ity against the art of the cinema. Archy reports that when
they left Hollywood Mehitabel and seven platinum-
blonde kittens, who were attempting to follow her across
the desert . . . but here is the latest bulletin from Archy:

mehitabels third kitten succumbed
to a scorpion today
poor little thing she said
i suppose the next one will perish

in a sandstorm and the next one
fall into the colorado river
it breaks my heart i am all
maternal instinct next to my art
as a modern dancer mother love is
the strongest thing in me
it is so strong that sometimes life seems to me
to be just one damned kitten
after another
but of course if i get back to broadway
without any kittens i will have more
freedom for my art
and can live my own life again
then she began to practice
dance steps among the cactus
casting fond eyes at a coyote

boss i am afraid
that mehitabels morals are no better
than before she struck hollywood
after all she remarked kittens
are but passing episodes in the life
of a great artist i may have been
given the bums rush from six auto camps
in three days but hells bells
i am still a lady

the loss of that kitten is a terrible grief
but an aristocrat and an artist

the retreat from hollywood

must bear up toujours gai
is my motto toujours gai

theres life in the old dame yet
and with that she cut a caper with
the heat at one hundred and forty
degrees fahrenheit

xlv

artists shouldnt have offspring

A bulletin from Archy the Cockroach, who started out last July to hitch-hike from Hollywood to New York with Mehitabel the Cat and Mehitabel's seven platinum-blonde kittens:

had a great break boss
got a ride on the running board of a car
and caught up with mehitabel
in new mexico where she is gadding about
with a coyote friend
i asked her where the kittens were
kittens said mehitabel kittens
with a puzzled look on her face

why goodness gracious i seem to remember
that i did have some kittens
i hope nothing terrible has happened
to the poor little things but if something has
i suppose they are better off
an artist like me shouldnt really
have offspring it handicaps her career
archy i want you to meet my boy friend
cowboy bill the coyote i call him
i am trying to get him to come to new york
with me and do a burlesque turn
isnt he handsome i said tactfully that he looked
very distinguished to me and all bill said
was nerts insect nerts

                archy

xlvi
what does a trouper care

A bulletin from Archy, who started weeks ago hitch-hiking across the country from California to New York, accompanied by Mehitabel and the seven platinum-blonde kittens she acquired in Hollywood:

> still somewhere in arizona
> sometime in october
> sand storm struck us yesterday
> i peeped out from under a rock
> and saw mehitabel dancing
> and singing as follows
> ive got a rock in my eye

and a scorpion in my gizzard
but what does an artist care
for a bit of red hot blizzard
my feet are full of cactus
there are blisters in my hair
but howl storm howl
what does a trouper care
i got a thirst like a mummy
i got a desert chill
but cheerio my deario
theres a dance in the old dame still
two more of the kittens disappeared
well i got three left said mehitabel
poor little dears i am afraid
they will never reach broadway
unless they learn how to get milk
from the cactus plants damn them
their appetites are spoiling my figure
a lot of encouragement a dancer gets
from her family i must say
any other artist i know would tell them
to go wean themselves on alkali
and be done with them but my great weakness
is my maternal instinct
boss i made nearly a mile today
before the sand storm blew me back
i hear texas is a thousand miles across

                            archy

xlvii
is a coyote a cat

Archy and Mehitabel are still plugging along valiantly, somewhere in Arizona. Archy reports that the seven platinum-blonde kittens with which Mehitabel left Hollywood have now been reduced to two.

He adds:

> please tell me whether
> a coyote is of the cat family or not
> mehitabel has been very friendly lately
> with a coyote
> she says he has only a fatherly interest
> she said the same thing in Hollywood
> and then came the kittens

the fifth one perished by the way
while trying to get milk
out of a cactus plant
i asked mehitabel today if she were
grieving for the other five
and she replied what other five
there is no doubt that mehitabel
has suffered a good deal
but one nice thing is that she does not
seem to remember it long

xlviii
human nature aint that bad

A bulletin from Archy, who is back in New York and
glad of it.

thought i would never get home
did i tell you about the two bums
i listened to in california
named spike and cheesy
they were washing selves and clothes
in an irrigation ditch
cheesy says this valley was once the bottom
of the ocean dont that give you a queer feeling
now i know why i feel at home here says spike
my old man always said I would sink lower
than any other human on earth
and it appears that i have attained my goal at last

the long struggle of my life has ended
in complete victory i am finally at
where i was going to please pass the canned heat
i want to drink to the boy who made good
i suppose said cheesy we have been getting
a lot of handouts and nickels
really intended for workingmen out of jobs
never look a gift horse in the mouth said spike
but what I am afraid of said cheesy
is that this depression will end some time
and people will start offering me jobs again
cheer up said spike dont be a pessimist
we weathered lots of good times before
and we will manage to get through somehow
when they come again
you gotta look on the bright side of things
this depression is making the public gift minded
i dont know said cheesy i am scared
it will be just hell for me
when prosperity returns with an open job
on every four corners
listen said spike you are plain selfish
dont you know there are a lot of people
in this world who really like to work
cheesy took the canned heat and thought and thought
and thought and thought before he spoke again
i dont believe it he said finally
after all human nature aint that bad

archy

xlix
could such things be

A bulletin from Archy, who, with Mehitabel the Cat, started out last July to hitch-hike from Hollywood to New York:

well boss here i am back in new york
i got a great break
after walking for months through arizona
i caught a ride on an airplane
and the first person i saw here was mehitabel
who had bummed her way
in a tourist trailer
she is living in shinbone alley
on second hand fish heads she drags away

from the east side markets
and she has some new kittens
they are the most peculiar kittens i ever saw
not the ones she left hollywood with
months ago or anything like them
there are five of these new ones
and they dont mew
they make a noise more like barking
i thought of that coyote she was so friendly with
in the southwest but i did not ask
any tactless questions
boss do you suppose such things could be

                                    archy

1
be damned mother dear

Mehitabel the Cat is still living in Shinbone Alley with the strange kittens which arrived shortly after Mehitabel's arrival from the Southwest. Archy, the Cockroach, says ... but let him tell it:

> one of mehitabels kittens
> licked a bull pup yesterday
> and she is very proud
> but hang them she says
> i cant teach them to fight like cats
> i told one of them yesterday
> when i left home
> i might bring him back
> a pretty neck ribbon
> if he was a good kitten

and he answered me in a strange voice
ribbon be damned mother dear
what i want is a brass collar
with spikes on it
and another one whom i had been
calling pussy says to me
pussy be damned mother dear
call me fido and another one
who got hold of a ball of catnip
complained it made him
sick at the stomach he says
catnip be damned mother dear
what i want is a bone to gnaw
what do you suppose makes them
act so strange archy
do you suppose i answered her
that prenatal influence
could have anything to do with it
perhaps that is it
she replied innocently
i seem to remember
that i was chased through
arizona and new mexico
by a coyote or did i dream
i will say you were chased
i told her my advice
is to rent them out
to a dog and pony show

                       archy

li
the artist always pays

boss i visited mehitabel last night
at her home in shinbone alley
she sat on a heap of frozen refuse
with those strange new kittens she has
frolicking around her
and sang a little song at the cold moon
which went like this

i have had my ups i have had my downs
i never was nobodys pet
i got a limp in my left hind leg
but theres life in the old dame yet

my first boy friend was a maltese tom
quite handsomely constructed
i trusted him but the first thing i knew
i was practically abducted

then i took up with a persian prince
a cat by no means plain
and that exotic son of a gun
abducted me again

what chance has an innocent kitten got
with the background of a lady
when feline blighters betray her trust
in ways lowlifed and shady

my next boy friend was a yellow bum
who loafed down by the docks
i rustled that gonifs rats for him
and he paid me with hard knocks

i have had my ups i have had my downs
i have led a helluva life
it was all these abductions unsettled my mind
for being somebodys wife

today i am here tomorrow flung
on a scow bound down the bay
but wotthehell o wotthehell
i m a lady thats toujours gai

the artist always pays

my next boy friend was a theater cat
a kind of a backstage pet
he taught me to dance and get me right
theres a dance in the old dame yet

my next boy friend he left me flat
with a family and no milk
and i says to him as i lifted his eye
i ll learn ye how to bilk

i have had my ups i have had my downs
i have been through the mill
but in spite of a hundred abductions kid
i am a lady still

my next friend wore a ribbon and bells
but he laughed and left me broke
and i said as i sliced him into scraps
laugh off this little joke

some day my guts will be fiddle strings
but my ghost will dance while they play
for they cant take the pep from the old girls soul
and i am toujours gai

my heart has been broken a thousand times
i have had my downs and ups
but the queerest thing ever happened to me
is these kittens as turned out pups

o wotthehell o toujours gai
i never had time to fret
i danced to whatever tune was played
and theres life in the old dame yet

i have had my ups i have had my downs
i have been through the mill
but i said when i clawed that coyotes face
thank god i am a lady still

and then she added looking at those
extraordinary kittens of hers
archy i wish you would
take a little trip up to the zoo
and see if they have any department there
for odd sizes and new species

i got to find a home
for these damned freaks somewhere
poor little things my heart bleeds for them
it agonizes my maternal instinct
one way or another an artist always pays

                                    archy

lii

maternal care

i was down in shinbone alley
yesterday on a visit
to mehitabel and her queer kittens
the ones which came
to her maternal care
after her journey through the southwest
damn them archy she said to me
i cant teach them to purr
and mew like kittens should
they only growl and bark
and yesterday the five of them
raided a butcher shop

around the corner and came home
with a whole lamb
and a cop chasing them
they turned on him
and tore half his clothes off of him
and he went away howling
that he would probably have
hydrophobia
archy they dont take after
any of my folks at all
i am beginning to think
they are a bunch of wild dogs
what have i ever done
to have these offspring wished on me
poor mehitabel
she gets such bad breaks
but wot the hell archy wot the hell
she says my motto is toujours gai
i may have made a false step or two
but i am always the lady
and theres a dance or two
in the old dame yet

                                    archy

liii

to hell with anything common

well boss what should i see
last evening but our old friend
mehitabel the cat
she was finishing a fish head
she had dragged out of a garbage can
one of her eyes
was bloodshot but the other
glowed with the old
unconquerable lustre
there was a drab and ashen look
about her fur
but her step is swift and wiry

and her brave tail is still
a joyous banner in the air
has life been using you hard
mehitabel i asked her
pretty rough little cockroach
says she but what the hell
what the hell
toujours gai is my motto
always game and always gay
what the hell archy
theres a life or two
in the old girl yet i
am always jolly archy
and always the lady
what the hell
they cant take that away
from me archy
and always free archy
i live my own life archy
and i shall right up to the moment
the d s c wagon gets me
and carts me to the garbage scow
archy you may not believe it
but last week i received no less
than three offers of permanent homes
all from very respectable cats
with ribbons around their necks
but nothing doing
on this domesticity stuff

to hell with anything common

i am a free spirit
i am of royal descent archy
my grandmother was a persian
princess and i cant see myself
falling for any bourgeois
apartment house stuff
either a palace or else
complete liberty for me
i play a lone hand
and i never take up with tame toms
my particular friends have always
been very gentlemanly cats archy
to hell with anything common archy
that has always been my motto
always gay and always the lady
you cant trust half
of these damned pet cats
anyhow they will double cross
a lady with no conscience
only last week i was singing
on a back fence and one of these
dolled up johnnies came out of the
    basement
and joined me he had a silver bell on
kid he says to me i fall for you
why you sudden thing says i
i like your nerve
come live with me and be my love
says he and i will show you how

to pick open the ice box door
sweet thing says i
your line of talk convinces me
that we are affinities lead me to
the cream pitcher
i followed this slick crook
into the kitchen and just as we got
the ice box door open in came
the cook what does he do but pretend
he never knew me and she hits me
in the slats with a flat iron
was that any way to treat a lady
archy that cheap johnnie had
practically abducted me as you might
     say
and then deserted me
but what the hell archy what
the hell i am too much
the lady to beef about it
i laid for him in the alley
the next night and tore one of his
ears into fringes and lifted
an eye out of him now you
puzzle faced four flusher i told him
that will teach you how to
double cross a lady
always game and always gay
archy that is me what the hell
theres a dance or two

in the old dame yet
class is the thing that counts
archy you cant get away
from class

well boss i think that in spite
of her brave words and gallant
spirit our friend mehitabel
is feeling her years and constant
exposure to the elements
another year and i will likely
see her funeral cortege
winding through the traffic
a line of d s c wagons headed
for the refuse scows and poor
mehitabel ashily stark
in the foremost cart

        archy

liv
a word from little archibald

thank you
for the mittens
socks and
muffler for me
knitted out of
frogs hair by one
of my admirers which
you so kindly
forwarded i suppose
the reason
i got them was that
they were too

small for you
to wear yourself
yours for rum
crime and riot

archy